School is out for the summer and Fuego shouts, "Woo Hoo! This summer will be SO MUCH FUN! And summer camp is just a few weeks away!"

He was thinking of how he would spend time staying cool during the hot Texas summer: floating in the swimming pool, sailing down the waterslides, and going horseback riding, just to name a few. He's been dreaming of the many adventures that await him.

FUEGO | Super Power

© 2020 Pam White

All rights reserved. This book or parts thereof may not be reproduced in any form, stored in any retrieval system, or transmitted in any form by any means—electronic, mechanical, photocopy, recording, or otherwise—without prior written permission of the publisher, except as provided by United States of America copyright law. For permission requests, write to the publisher, at "Attention: Permissions Coordinator," at the email address below.

ISBN - 978-1-5323-9358-7

Illustrated by Justin Stewart
Justifii.com

For information about special discounts available for bulk purchases, sales promotions, fund-raising and educational needs, contact Pam White at pam@fuegokids.com

Before Fuego leaves for camp, to his surprise some unexpected plans are being discussed among several of his friends. Friends he has known and grown up with all of his life are taking a turn for the worst. Their idea of summer fun has gone to a new level. They have decided to take up stealing, and they want Fuego to join them.

All four of his best friends were planning to take part in stealing from their neighborhood toy store. Spike was the leader, then BJ, Mitch, and Jake were also on board with this crazy idea. It isn't because they don't have enough toys. It's because they love the excitement! They want an adventure!

Fuego knew stealing was wrong. How could he stand up for what was right, when his friends are following each other and doing wrong? Fuego has a conversation with God, "Wow, I just don't know what to do. How can I explain to my friends that this is wrong?"

Fuego's friends are planning to meet at Spike's house next Saturday at 10:00am. He thought to himself, "That's only a week away. What should I do? What will I say to them? How can I get out of this situation?"

The pressure of what to do became so overwhelming to Fuego. He didn't know where to turn for help. He thought about talking to his Mom or Dad, or even his Sunday school teacher. But he was afraid. So instead, he decided to pack his bag and run away.

Somehow Fuego lost sight that he had the power of God inside of him to stand up against peer pressure.* You see, when he was 8 years old, he had received the first gift when he made a decision to live for Jesus. The gift of salvation,* and the forgiveness of his sins.* But there was MORE...

*Peer pressure - When your circle of friends influence the decisions you make. They want you to do what they do, whether the decision is right, wrong, good, or bad.

*Salvation - The gift of "life" from God. Once you receive Jesus as leader of your life, your name is written in the "book of life".

*Sins - Wrong things you have done that go against what the Bible teaches. It is also knowing what is right, and not doing it. Everyone has a sin nature until made right with God through salvation.

At the age of 10, Fuego received the second gift, the gift of the Holy Spirit. He received a new prayer language, called tongues.* When filled with the Holy Spirit he received the POWER to live for God and to say no to temptation.*

Fuego didn't have a plan for where he would stay after running away. He was just following his feelings on the inside. Thoughts of fear were overtaking him!

*Temptation - A strong desire to do something. Usually this is a desire to do something you should NOT do. (Example: You don't have money, but YOU want a piece of candy SO bad. You can't stop thinking about putting it in your pocket!)

*Tongues - A heavenly language given to you by the Holy Spirit for the purpose of prayer, joy, and comfort. (Mark 16:7, Acts 1:8, Acts 2:4, Acts 8:15-17, Acts 19:6)

Fuego ran as far as the outskirts of town and found a long stretch of railroad tracks. He decided it would be a good place to walk and think. There was no one in sight for miles, and as he continued to walk, he began to hear a quiet voice on the inside. The voice was so quiet, it was almost a whisper: "You are more than a conqueror through Jesus Christ! No weapon formed against you shall prosper! Greater is He that is in you than he that is in the world! You can do all things through Christ who strengthens you!"

An excitement rose up on the inside of Fuego. It was the Spirit of God bringing back the Bible verses he had learned in children's church. God was speaking to him through the scriptures about his situation. It no longer mattered what his friends would think of him; he wanted to stand for what was right.

Fuego began to talk to God, "Lord I am sorry for running away and forgetting that you are ALWAYS with me. The Bible says you will NEVER leave me, even in the hard times."

Suddenly he could feel a confidence rise up like a GIANT on the inside of him! He was ready to go back now and face what he feared most! He began running back home, as fast as his feet would take him. When Fuego arrived home, he asked his parents to forgive him for running away. The joy of living life and having adventures suddenly returned to his heart!

You can receive this same POWER from the Holy Spirit that Fuego experienced. The proof of the Holy Spirit being on the inside of you will show up as a new language for prayer. You can read about it in the book of Acts in the Holy Bible.

Just pray this prayer:

Dear Lord Jesus, thank you for being Lord of my life. I now want to receive the power of the Holy Spirit to be able to live boldly for you, to stand against temptation, to be a witness to others, and to live a life of victory! Fill me with the Holy Spirit. I receive this special gift you have for me with the proof of speaking in other tongues. In Jesus' Name, amen.

The POWER of the Holy Spirit is on the inside of YOU! Open your mouth and your lips and use your voice to begin speaking in your new prayer language. Don't be afraid. God has not given you a spirit of fear. Now you've got it! Now you have the POWER to live for God!

And by the way, Fuego was ready to meet his friends on that Saturday morning. He had a new goal in mind. It was to encourage his friends to serve God, and God would make sure they had a fun and memorable summer. He convinced them to go to church camp with him, instead of stealing and getting into trouble.

And they ALL did! They had a summer of adventure! Each one of them made a decision to serve God, and they were ALL filled with the Holy Spirit!

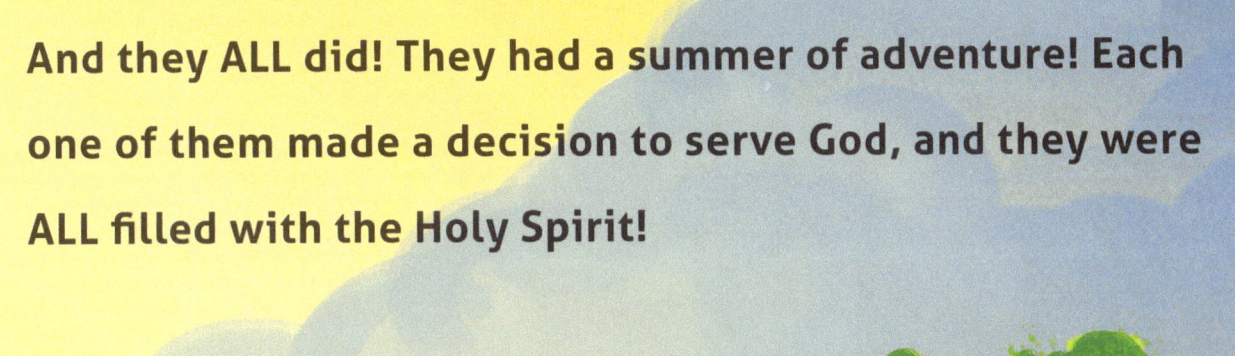

NOTE FROM THE AUTHOR: PAM WHITE

The enemy is not people, or your friends; it's the devil. You can't see him but he is real. He wants to keep you from living the plan God has for your life. He will try to place obstacles in your way to keep you from serving God or cause you to blame God for the bad things that happen. Remember that God is ALWAYS GOOD, and he loves you ALL the time! Don't forget to pray in your new prayer language every day. The Holy Spirit is the teacher, comforter, and encourager. You may go through difficult times in life, but remember, "YOU HAVE THE POWER" of the Holy Spirit within you, to help you through every situation! Now is a good time to read from your Bible in the book of Acts, chapters 1, 2, 8, and 19.

SCRIPTURES FOR CONFESSION (NLT)

Here are some scriptures from the Bible for you to practice reading out loud every day. They will come back to your memory when you need them the most. Just like the Holy Spirit reminded Fuego of scriptures he had learned in children's church when he was afraid of facing his friends and doing what was right, He will help you, too!

"I will pay attention and listen carefully to God's words. I will not lose sight of them. They will penetrate deep into my heart, for they bring life to me and healing to my whole body. I will guard my heart above all else, for it determines the course of my life." Proverbs 4:20-23

"For I can do everything through Christ, who gives me strength." Philippians 4:13

"No, despite all these things, overwhelming victory is mine through Christ, who loved me." Romans 8:37

"The thief's purpose is to steal and kill and destroy. Jesus' purpose is to give me a rich and satisfying life." John 10:10

"I will stay pure by obeying God's word. I will not wonder from your commands. I have hidden your word in my heart, that I might not sin against you." Psalm 119:9-11

"Your word is a lamp to guide my feet and a light for my path." Psalm 119:105

"For God knows the plans He has for me. They are plans for good and not for disaster, to give me a future and a hope." Jeremiah 29:11

"For God has not given me a spirit of fear and timidity, but of power, love, and self-discipline." 2 Timothy 1:7

CPSIA information can be obtained
at www.ICGtesting.com
Printed in the USA
BVHW022244231220
596378BV00001B/1